MARK MARTIN

Small Town Hero, Big League Racer

by

Kathy Persinger

SPORTS PUBLISHING L.L.C.
www.SportsPublishingLLC.com

Production manager: Susan Moyer
Project manager: Jim Henehan
Developmental editor: Lynnette Bogard
Cover design: Kerri Baker
Copy editor: Cynthia L. McNew

ISBN: 1-58382-654-X

NASCAR is a registered trademark of the National Association for Stock Car
Auto Racing, Inc.

Roush Racing's and Mark Martin's name and/or likeness used by authority of
Roush Racing, Livonia, Michigan. VIAGRA ® and the blue diamond tablet
shape are registered trademarks of Pfizer Inc. Used under license. Pfizer and the
blue diamond tablet shape are registered trademarks of Pfizer Inc. Used under
license.

SPORTS PUBLISHING L.L.C.
www.SportsPublishingLLC.com

Printed in the United States.

CONTENTS

Acknowledgments iv

Introduction vi

1 Roots 1

2 Family 11

3 1981 25

4 Roush Racing 33

5 Sponsorship 45

6 2001 vs. 2002 53

7 Matt 67

8 Statistics 77

Acknowledgments

Before the start of the 2002 NASCAR season, driver Mark Martin told an interviewer, "I'm a competitor. I want to win every pole, every race, every practice, you name it, but that's just not going to always happen. You can't control a flat tire here, or a part going bad there. There are so many things out there that you can't control."

What Mark can control is the way he prepares, and the way he can rely on more than two decades of experience behind a wheel, to produce a career that has amassed a huge fan base and down-to-earth appeal.

The only current NASCAR driver to have been born in Arkansas, Mark started learning his skills while in elementary school, determined to take his affection for speed as far as he could.

There are several people to thank for their help in putting this book together. First, to NASCAR beat reporter David Poole, based in Charlotte, North Carolina, for his guidance and encouragement. And to Paul Glover, sports editor of the *Batesville* (Arkansas) *Daily Guard* newspaper, for his reflections and hometown insight.

To Wayne Brooks, who built cars for Mark in the early years, raced with him, and knew Mark before he was old enough to drive legally: Thanks for the stories and wisdom about the sport, as it used to be and as it is.

And thanks to Larry Shaw, who also built the cars and spent his every weekend with the Martins, on the rural roads, traveling and hoping, years back.

Thanks to the friendly people at Roush Racing in Concord, North Carolina, who operate a new, massive complex dedicated to the sport. And to the many people who know Mark, for the tales they have to tell.

And to my children—Christopher, Sarah and Tyler—for their love and support.

INTRODUCTION

Mark Martin is not your typical 21st-century NASCAR driver. Born in 1959, he's more weathered than the circuit's crop of hot, young superstars, many of whom cite birth dates in the mid- to late 1970s.

He isn't sponsored by a popular beverage, or a home improvement company, or batteries or cell phones. His sponsor is a men's health product, prescription only.

He sports a crew cut, not tossable hair, like the youngsters, and, at five foot six and 150 pounds, he's one of the smaller guys out there. His face has wrinkles, and he doesn't mind if his eyes squint in the sun, on camera, framed by more lines instead of expensive designer shades.

He is married, with children.

And he doesn't live among the cluster of drivers and shops around Mooresville, Concord and Charlotte, North Carolina. He's from Batesville,

Arkansas, and lives in Daytona Beach, Florida, though his Roush Racing team is based in Concord.

Mark just happens to have a longer commute, when needed, to work.

"The whole world of motorsports is changing, and it will be dramatically different 10 years from now because of the influence of the younger drivers coming into the sport," Mark said in spring 2003.

So what is it about Mark Martin, driver of the No. 6 Ford Taurus, that makes him so enduringly popular?

Consistency, perhaps.

The records he's set.

And, maybe, it's that he's a family man, who proudly announces that his faith sustains him. He has roots.

"I'm happy with what I've been able to do," Mark said. "I don't think I'm the greatest race car driver that ever lived, but I've got a lot of nice trophies on the shelf."

In this book, we're going to see how they got there.

Come along for the trip as we follow Mark's career from driving the family truck at a young age, to hauling 18-wheelers cross-country, to gracing NASCAR's Victory Lane. He's had a good, fast ride.

YOU GO MARK WIN, WIN WIN!

Dinwiddie, Va.

—Inscription on a brick outside Roush Racing headquarters in Concord, North Carolina

Roots

The South has changed much since NASCAR driver Mark Martin was born on January 9, 1959, in Batesville, Arkansas.

Back then, Batesville had fewer than 1,000 homes. The city, about 85 miles northeast of the state capital of Little Rock, as the crow flies, and about 27 square kilometers in size, grew to nearly 9,500 residents by 2000.

Located along the White River, Batesville is known for its poultry production and as the home of three small colleges. It has three AM radio stations, one of which only airs during daylight, and two FM stations.

The Cleburne County Fair comes to nearby Heber Springs every September and has for 112 years. The city is up to four public elementary schools, two middle schools, a junior high and two high schools.

At the entrance to town, there's a sign that says "Home of NASCAR Champion Mark Martin," and the Old Independence Regional Museum, near Main Street, has some racing displays and information about the city's famous past resident.

But this small town near the base of the Ozark Mountains is still a sack of ZIP codes away from any big city.

Perhaps all this contributed to Mark's desire to steer a car competitively at age 15 before the state allowed that it was OK for him to roll down a highway. He ran on dirt, like the NASCAR pioneers before him, and more often than not, he won.

He even skipped his high school graduation ceremony to race, a night his former car builder, Larry Shaw, remembers.

(Photo courtesy of Jackie Martin)

By choice, Shaw said, Mark's high school years away from the classroom were spent in a garage, not in the social circle.

"That's all he ever did. He didn't do anything after school," Shaw said. "He didn't have girlfriends. You work all week on the race car, then you race. He never did really say it, but I think he got robbed of his high school days. But he just didn't have time for it. He couldn't wait for Friday night.

"Come graduation, they had a big race in Missouri, at the fairgrounds. They had Mark advertised real heavy to be there, but graduation or not, he was gonna be there."

Mark and his crew, during those years, took his machine to places such as the Benton Speed Bowl in Bryant, Arkansas, and Independence County Raceway in Batesville. He was a regular at the half-mile dirt track in Heber Springs, and as a high school senior he won a distance championship at Mo-Ark Raceway, a three-eighths-mile semi-banked clay oval over the line in West Plains, Missouri.

Mark needed a good rest after putting in a hard day as a cowboy. **(Photo courtesy of Jackie Martin)**

And he had what must have seemed to him like big sponsors—Gardner Trucking Company of Walterboro, South Carolina, and Continental Battery Company of Dallas, Texas.

"I didn't have a childhood," Mark said back in 2001. "I didn't have a teen age. I didn't do all those things that a lot of people do."

"Maybe it just shows some of the growing pains," said racing buddy Wayne Brooks of Bald Knob, Arkansas. "But I remember once he was upset, and he didn't have a driver's license, and it looked like he had a booster seat in his race car, and they were running these wood haulers out there.

"They would put their car on the back of a wood hauler and get it up to the track, and they got him out there one time and roughed him up and bumped him around a lot, and he comes in the pits and just kinda teared up a little bit, and ol' Julian [Mark's father] is sitting there talking to him a little bit.

"And Mark says he's going to pay those fellers back and give them some of their own stuff. He went out there and earned their respect."

Early problems or not, Mark kept wanting to race, Shaw said.

"My way of thinking is that Mark came on to this scene, and I feel like Mark was like running through a glass door telling other people they can start really young and do whatever they want to in life," Shaw said. "We thought it was impossible, and he did it.

"In about 1977, we went to Rockford, Illinois, to the national short track championship, and there he is, barely 17 years old, and there's over 200 cars trying to get into a 24-car field, and he sets the second quickest time and goes on to win the 400-lap race.

"We actually went up the year before, as fans, and it was so scary how fast it was, and we go up the next year and win. And when he accomplished that, there was no doubt in my mind he could do whatever he wanted to."

Said Brooks, who built and sold engines for Mark's cars: "Mark had a lot of natural talent… this sport was really young, and at that time there were

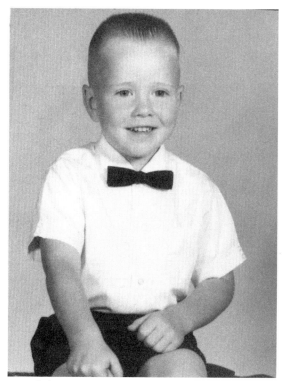

(Photo courtesy of Jackie Martin)

very few chassis builders, and now there are several companies in every state—but at that time we built everything ourselves. The driver had to do a lot. There was no power steering then, and Mark was a

Mark had an early interest in those "other" sports. (**Photo courtesy of Jackie Martin**)

little guy. You had to manhandle them things. They would run sideways around a race track, a little more out of control than they are now. But he had a lot of raw talent."

For Mark Martin, it would prove to be a talent that eventually would take him to the top of his sport.

MATT WYATT # 1
MARK MARTIN FAN
AGE 9

—Inscription on a brick outside Roush Racing

Family

Imagine being five years old, too young to cross the street by yourself, and too small to reach the cookie jar on the counter. Now imagine being five years old and standing on the driver's seat of a speeding rocket, clenching the steering wheel, while your daddy pushes the gas pedal, faster and faster, begging you not to wreck, not to hit the ditches, the fences, the obstructions of your back-country race course.

This is how Mark Martin learned to drive, from his dad, Julian, who put his son behind a wheel as soon as he was old enough to grasp it in his hands.

Car builder Larry Shaw remembers hearing the story. "It was an old pickup truck," Shaw said. "They

Even at an early age, Mark had some big boots to fill.
(Photo courtesy of Jackie Martin)

were about 15 miles from Batesville, in Cleburne County, and he told Mark to take the steering wheel and drive it. And he said, 'No, I don't want to.' And Julian said, 'If you don't take it, we're gonna crash.' That was before I knew them."

Julian Martin. **(Photo courtesy of Jackie Martin)**

Julian Martin owned a trucking company. Driving was inevitable for Mark, and it soon became the family's passion.

Shaw hooked up with the Martins by 1970 as a friend, and by 1973 they were building race cars together. "For the next five or six years, we were with each other night and day," he said. "We didn't have time to do anything but work on the race car."

Racing took over their lives. It was what they did, what they lived for.

"When they started racing, I had been racing a couple or three years, and I had been friends with Julian and Mark," said friend Wayne Brooks, also a driver and 10 years older than Mark. "Basically, I just helped them out. We raced at the local dirt tracks around Arkansas. They were having problems keeping motors together, and at the time I was building race car engines, and I sold them an engine.

"In fact, I believe Mark won his first race with that motor, but I can't swear to that. About a season later, I sold him my race car, which was kinda dominant at the time. And I moved to the next class, and Mark had a good year or so with that."

What Mark had was a 1955, six-cylinder, yellow Chevrolet, painted with the number 37. He later bought a white '55 Chevy from Brooks, with the number 2 on the side, a number that would be

Julian Martin. **(Photo courtesy of Jackie Martin)**

important, though he didn't know it, many years later with his son Matt.

"He never did say, 'I got a race car, and you don't.' It never did come up," Shaw said. "And actually the people we raced then, here's Mark 13 or 14, and we raced people 25 to 50. Mark was good. The cocky side of him never did come out."

In 2001, Mark was going through a difficult season, and he finished 12th in the NASCAR championship standings, the lowest placing since his 15th in 1988. The hardship caused him to reflect on where he was, where he came from, what he wanted from the sport of racing and what his family meant—his father's influence on him and his influence on his son's promising career.

"Nobody said I had to race the car when my dad died—I said I had to," Mark said after his father, stepmother and half-sister were killed in a plane crash in 1998. "As long as I'm committed to something, I'm not staying home—for anything. I won't miss a race for anything. Broken bones, broken in half, it doesn't matter—I'm in there, I'm driving."

(Photo courtesy of Jackie Martin)

He wanted to carry on what his father taught him.

The Julian Martin Trucking Company ran 18-wheelers, and the father was intent on passing his driving skills to his son. So when Mark was five, his dad began teaching him the basics, instilling a passion in the child to guide anything with wheels—bicycles, motorcycles, cars, trucks.

Sometimes Mark, barely old enough to read and write, would stand in the seat in front of his dad, and Julian would push the pedals as Mark steered, 75 miles per hour along the gravel roads around Batesville. He made Mark do the work, just as he had done years before with Mark's older sister, Glenda, and they'd tease the corners and the fences and fate and always come out ahead.

"I gave him a lot of room. I let him do things, sometimes when he was too young," Julian Martin stated in a book about his son.

"And fortunately he didn't kill himself or tear too much up. He handled it real well. If you give a kid a lot of rope, and they don't kill themselves, that works real good."

When Mark was 15, still too young for a license, his father would let him drive the big rigs while he napped in the sleeper compartment.

Once a year, they'd haul a refrigerated truck from Batesville to California, to fetch fresh produce during the harvest season. Much of the trip, Mark was at the controls, even though he needed a booster seat

Mark's sister, Glenda Martin. **(Photo courtesy of Jackie Martin)**

and a little luck with grasping the big wheel. He drove a truck that, of the 35 in the company's fleet, was his. Julian Martin rigged it to go faster than any other truck on his lot. On a good day, the vehicle could hit 80 miles per hour.

But fast trucking wasn't Mark's top career choice. He needed something smaller and much faster.

Shaw helped Mark and Julian build that first race car, with the words "Martin Trucking" on the front left panel. The driver's seat was placed toward the center of the dash, a plan to keep him safer.

On April 12, 1974, Mark drove that car in his first race, at a place called Locust Grove. Seven days later, in the second race of his career, he won, at the same track.

The urge to drive and succeed had been passed down.

The family still owns the trucking company.

Glenda Martin-White, Mark's sister, helps run the business, now J-Mar Express, in Searcy, Arkansas. And Mark cruises in from time to time.

Jackie Martin. (Photo courtesy of Jackie Martin)

"He visits here on a few occasions, but he's like most people who are involved in NASCAR, very busy," said Paul Glover, sports editor of the Batesville newspaper. "He's been here a few times for some promotional things, and he's been here for his family from time to time. He's always nice, and very accommodating, but he's very busy."

Arkansas had provided the beginning, but there was much more to do.

For Mark, the route from Batesville to NASCAR was in high gear.

MARK MARTIN
A CLEAN DRIVER!

Gary D. Vallow

—***Inscription on a brick outside Roush Racing***

CHAPTER THREE

1981

Mark showed up on the NASCAR Cup scene for the first time in 1981, as a driver/owner. He ran only five races that year, finishing 42nd in NASCAR championship points. He came in third at the race in Martinsville, and he was on the pole at Nashville and Richmond.

In his first career start at North Wilkesboro, he started fifth and finished 27th.

His luck would get better.

"Julian really helped surround Mark with good people," said friend Wayne Brooks. "From the day he started, he taught Mark that you have to be around the best, the right people, to do what they've

Mark sitting on his ASA car before qualifying in late 1970s with longtime crew chief David Lovendahl in background. After Mark failed to make it in NASCAR competition the first time, he went back to ASA. When he came back, it was in a NASCAR Busch Series car in 1987 owned by Lovendahl's brother-in-law Bruce Lawmaster. **(Photo by Dick Conway)**

Mark gets loose and scrapes the guardrail at the old Richmond Fairgrounds half-mile track in a 1982 NASCAR race. Mark had carried the number 2 on his ASA cars, and since it was already taken by another team in NASCAR Cup, he ran the 02. (**Photo by Dick Conway**)

accomplished. It don't matter if you're talking about Dale [Earnhardt] Junior or if you're talking about [Michael] Waltrip; they have to have the right people around them."

A young Mark Martin in the pits with two NASCAR legends, David Pearson and short track ace Butch Lindley, a two-time NASCAR Sportsman Series champion. Butch Lindley eventually died in 1990 after a five-year coma that he sustained from racing injuries in a crash in Bradenton, Florida, in 1985. **(Photo by Dick Conway)**

The following year, Mark showed the crowd he was ready to be noticed. He had eight top 10 finishes, even though he was funding his ride without a sponsor.

Things were going well, but they were about to go downhill.

Sitting with his Apache Stoves crew prior to a 1982 NASCAR race. Things were more casual in those days, with drivers hanging out in the pits and not sequestered in haulers and motor coaches. **(Photo by Dick Conway)**

Mark's luck ran out in 1983, and he auctioned off everything in his NASCAR shop. It was time for a change.

For two years, Mark stayed away from NASCAR, returning to the American Speed Association (ASA).

Already with an ASA championship under his belt at a young age, Mark poses beside his team's truck in the late 1970s. Notice the Dennis the Menace-like figure on the truck has an ASA champion patch on his uniform along with Mark's ASA car number 2. (**Photo by Dick Conway**)

He had started his career on asphalt in 1976, running in the V-8 class. In 1977, when he was old enough, he joined the ASA tour, racing against such drivers as Rusty Wallace and Bobby Allison. He was

Rookie of the Year and went on to win three more championships in 1978, 1979 and 1980.

After all that, he thought he was ready for the NASCAR Cup Series.

He wasn't.

After the auction, he landed back in ASA in 1984, 1985 and 1986. He met crew chief Jimmy Fennig in 1985, and the two won the '86 championship.

By 1987, though, Mark was running a full season in the NASCAR Busch Series.

It was then that Mark met someone who would become one of the most important people in his life.

His name was Jack Roush.

THE CAT IN THE HAT
ENGINE BUILDER
THE MAN JACK ROUSH

—Inscription on a brick outside Roush Racing

Roush Racing

On Aviation Boulevard in Concord, North Carolina, just past the mega-mall and clutter of restaurants, the landscape returns to cornfields and wooden fences along a two-lane road. Aside from the Depot Self Storage, not much is on this strip of pavement, until you get to the right turn and the street sign that reads Roush Place.

There on 25 acres are the new museum and world headquarters—a half-dozen buildings, cream-colored with dark-glass windows—to honor the empire that team owner Jack Roush built. Outside the three-story, 83,000-square-foot main building is a round, black marble fountain, with "ROUSH"

(Photo by Action Sports Photography Inc.)

mounted in the center in large, silver letters. On
the sidewalk around the fountain, forming a "Circle
of Fans," are personalized bricks, with engraved
messages.

(Photo by Action Sports Photography Inc.)

With three lines of space and room for 45 letters, the bricks offer support to Roush drivers, to the man himself, even to racing events. Names are etched in from the far reaches of the country.

There is even one not related to Roush's company or his brand of cars. It says:

(Photo by Dick Conway)

EARNHARDT 4EVER
MICHAEL BURNETT
ABBOT MAINE #3

Mark joined the Roush team in 1988, a move
that would thrust his career rapidly toward where
he wanted it to be. Roush noticed Mark in 1987,
when he drove in the NASCAR Busch Series, and
when Roush decided to form his own NASCAR

(Photo by Action Sports Photography Inc.)

Cup team for 1988, Mark was chosen to be the driver.

He's in good company, with teammates Greg Biffle, Matt Kenseth, Kurt Busch, Jeff Burton, Jon Wood and Carl Edwards.

Mark was 15th in points that first year, with 10 top 10 finishes, including a second at Bristol.

Going into the 2003 season, Mark had started 473 consecutive NASCAR Cup races, dating to February 18, 1988.

He had found his path.

It only took Mark until October of 1989 to find Victory Lane, when he took the checkered flag at the North Carolina Speedway in Rockingham.

By 1990, he was second in points, finishing 26 behind the late Dale Earnhardt, and had claimed victories at Richmond, North Wilkesboro and Michigan. He was sixth in 1991, when he won five poles, and won five races in 1993, including four in a row—at Watkins Glen, Bristol, Michigan and Darlington. He also won $1.65 million.

Jack and Mark have an amazing amount of respect for each other. **(Photo by Action Sports Photography Inc.)**

In 1994, Mark was second overall, again to Earnhardt. And in 1995, he proved his overall skill with four victories at four types of tracks, the "restrictor plate required" superspeedway at Talladega, the road course at Watkins Glen, the short track at North Wilkesboro, and the unrestricted superspeedway at Charlotte. The victory at Watkins

Glen made him the first NASCAR Cup driver to win three races there in a row.

Mark won four poles in 1996, including both Bristol races. And with his International Race of Champions victories in 1994, 1996, 1997 and 1998, he became the only driver to claim four IROC titles.

(Photo by Action Sports Photography Inc.)

In 1998, he won the most races of his career for one season, with seven, and the most money for a season, with more than $4 million.

He won twice in 1999 and finished third in points for the fourth time.

Then in 2001, he captured his 40th career pole, at Bristol, and his 41st at Richmond. He had 15 top 10s, but was 12th in points. He was determined to do better.

"What you can do is try to squeeze every bit of performance out of what you have every single time we put [the car] on the race track," Martin said. "I'm concentrating on trying to win races in 2002."

The 2002 season proved he wasn't in a slump, as he may have believed, and he rebounded to finish second behind Tony Stewart. He also won $5,279,400 and posted his 220th career top five NASCAR Cup finish and his 315th top 10.

He also had a new crew chief, Ben Leslie, who replaced Jimmy Fennig.

"It's been surprising. We really figured it would be more of an uphill battle to get going with the new team," said first-year car chief Todd Zeigler. "But it's been a lot easier than we expected."

FOR ALL RACE FANS WE LOST ON *9-11-01*

—Inscription on a brick outside Roush Racing

CHAPTER FIVE

Sponsorship

Mark's car is sponsored by Pfizer. "It's a prescription drug company that produces drugs for people who have health problems," Mark explained in 2001.

At every race through the 2003 season, a 50-foot mobile health unit owned by Pfizer Corporation parked in a lot near the track. It was called the "Tune Up For Life" hauler, and it offered race fans such things as blood pressure and cholesterol checks and glucose tests. It also offered a questionnaire that would help them in other areas of their lives.

When the program ended at the end of the 2003 season more than 125,000 people had received free

***Mark's sponsor has helped thousands of race fans through
its "Tune Up for Life" program.* (Photo by Action Sports
Photography Inc.)**

(Photo by Action Sports Photography Inc.)

health screenings compliments of Pfizer, since the program begain in 2000.

"Just like everybody else, [Pfizer] was marketing a product at the race track," Mark explained. "But they were giving race fans free physicals and health checks. A lot of these people wouldn't take off from work to go sit in a doctor's office to have a check-up. When you're over 35 years old…they needed to be going regularly. And they wouldn't."

The whole process took about 10 minutes—little more than it takes to seek out a souvenir from a NEXTEL spokesperson, a soft drink supplier, or other vendors who compete for fans' attention.

Geoff Cook, who works for Pfizer, is glad to have Mark's car take his company's name for a ride. "It should be seen as a sign of strength and intelligence," he said. "But there is this cultural

(Photo by Action Sports Photography Inc.)

(Photo by Action Sports Photography Inc.)

perspective of being a strong man and not needing to see a doctor. It doesn't make any sense at all."

Mark said, "It meant a lot when my sponsor was giving free health screenings to my fans and everyone else's fans. I get stuff all the time like, 'You saved my daddy's life,' or whatever. Or, 'Because of you, my dad went to the trailer and found out he was on the verge of having a stroke.' That means something."

YOU'RE MY IDOL
MARK MARTIN
J.J. PETERSON

—Inscription on a brick outside Roush Racing

2001 VS. 2002

"In my entire racing career, I've never had a year where I was not competitive," Mark said after the 2001 season. "But last season there were times when we just were not. I've run for 25 years, and it's just hard to say why that happens."

Mark won more than $3 million in 2001 and was on the pole for two races. He had three top five finishes and 15 top 10s. For many, that would be a good year. But Mark didn't like it, mainly because of two other numbers—he was never first, and he finished 12th in the NASCAR Cup points race.

(Photo by Action Sports Photography Inc.)

After four starts in 2001, he was 25th in the standings, with only one top 10.

"If we can get started on a roll, we'll be back to our old selves in no time," he said then. "We are working on some issues that have affected the team, but it takes time to work things out."

(Photo by Action Sports Photography Inc.)

Jimmy Fennig, Mark's former crew chief had big dreams for the season, like maybe opening with a victory in the Daytona 500, as he did when he was Bobby Allison's crew chief in 1988. "I know it would mean a lot to Mark," he said then.

(Photo by Action Sports Photography Inc.)

(Photo by Action Sports Photography Inc.)

But Mark completed only 175 of the 200 laps at his hometown track and finished 33rd, putting him 32nd overall to start the season.

Race after race, Victory Lane went unvisited by the No. 6 Ford and its crew.

(Photo by Action Sports Photography Inc.)

He was 20th at Rockingham the week after Daytona, the sport's first race following Dale Earnhardt's death. He was 41st two weeks later at Atlanta. He was 18th at the midseason stop in New Hampshire. The best moments came at Talladega, with a fourth-place run, and another fourth in the May race at Lowe's Motor Speedway near Charlotte.

He finished the season with a ninth place at New Hampshire in November, a race rescheduled because of the events of September 11.

"Some people think that I race to just run in circles out there on the track. But that is just not the case at all," Mark said. "I race and live to run good out there on the track. Just being out there is not what does it for me. It's running the best you can and competing."

In December, Roush Racing made a change. Ben Leslie, crew chief since April 2001 for Kurt Busch, came on to lead Mark's team after coaching Busch's car to five top 10s. Fennig became Busch's crew chief.

Leslie had been around racing for a while—15 years—and also had worked for Johnny Benson and Matt Kenseth. Plus, he and Mark were old friends, with Leslie having been Mark's mechanic and rear-tire changer in 1997 and on the crew for his NASCAR Busch Series cars for three years.

Two longtime racing guys, together on a mission.

(Photo by Action Sports Photography Inc.)

Mark developed a steely determination early in his career.
(Photo by Action Sports Photography Inc.)

"Just to be able to feed off the experience of a veteran like Mark will be a great experience for me," Leslie said after getting the job.

Two old friends, one common goal.

"We are looking for some wins in 2002," Leslie said. "I don't know if that is two wins or 10 wins, but ultimately we want to be in the hunt for the championship in November."

Part of their dream came true. The pair won only once, in the Coca-Cola 600 at Lowe's Motor Speedway, but finished the year with 22 top 10s, including 12 top fives.

Mark closed the season with three consecutive top fives to take second in points, only 38 behind NASCAR Cup champion Tony Stewart. Mark had been second at the midpoint of the season, too, after a second at Pocono and a fifth at the Pepsi 500 in Daytona. After the fall race at New Hampshire, he briefly became the points leader—the first time since the spring of 2000.

There were nine races remaining.

(Photo by Action Sports Photography Inc.)

"I really didn't expect to be contending for a championship with the [crew] changes that we made," Mark said after the season. "I hoped they would bring success and improvement, and it's been really, really good, but I don't think we expected this just yet."

Mark finished the season with a fourth-place drive at Homestead. His winnings for the year came to $5,251,905.

"We really fought for it, and you can't say that we ever gave up," he said after that race.

Two friends, one new team, one common goal. And a whole different season from the year before.

"It's progressed much faster than I ever imagined," Leslie said.

SIXAHOLIC
ALAN PANKOFF
CANADA

—*Inscription on a brick outside Roush Racing*

Matt

Sometimes, when a child grows up watching a parent's success at a sport, the only desired career choice is to follow.

NASCAR's most prominent examples are Dale Earnhardt Jr., son of the late seven-time champion Dale Earnhardt Sr., and Kyle Petty, son of seven-time champion Richard Petty.

And then, there is—or will be—Matt Martin.

Matt, born in December, 1991, is the youngest of the Martins' five children (his four sisters were born in the 1970s).

The first thought is that he's just a regular kid. He uses typical preteen expressions, such as "It's

(Photo by Steven Rose/MMP Inc.)

tight" or "It's the bomb." He once visited the Dallas Cowboys' locker room, and critiqued the experience by saying it needed a slushie machine. He likes math in school, hair gel and football.

That is where any similarities between Matt Martin and his peers end.

He'd rather drive.

With the tools of his apparent trade spread before him, Matt has taken any other common traits he has to boys his age and pushed them aside.

But driving did not happen in the reckless way his father was introduced to speed, at the controls of a monstrous, roaring 18-wheeler, or by standing on the seat to grasp the wheel of a swerving family pickup. No, Matt took on the sport by racing quarter midgets in 1999 at age seven. With his father Mark encouraging him, he advanced to Bandoleros and to testing Legends cars.

In 2003, he signed a contract with Ford Motor Company, the youngest driver ever to clinch a sponsorship deal with the company.

Matt Martin poses with his Bandolero car. **(Photo by Steven Rose/MMP Inc.)**

"For people who might get tunnel vision about whatever things they're doing in life, being able to do what I do with Matt and his racing keeps me in touch with what is truly important," Mark told an interviewer early in the 2003 season. "It enables me to maintain a focus on what I'm doing with my career, but at the same time it makes you well rounded because there are a lot of other things in life that are important, too."

Mark sees a parallel in the way he and his son learned to drive. But he also sees a detachment in the methods.

"My father and I had a special relationship and a love for things that went fast," Mark said. "But today is completely different. Matt started racing when he was seven years old. I didn't start racing until I was a teenager. I didn't even have a motorcycle when I was the age that Matt started at. Matt is not consumed by racing, as I was when I was younger. He is more diverse, and he has different interests than I did in other things as well.

"From my perspective, I try to share and get involved in as much of that as I can and feel like that's a benefit to both of us."

Some of the benefits of being the talented son of a NASCAR star have created a lengthy, impressive resume.

In 1998, Matt took Jeff Gordon's original quarter midget car for a test drive at Lowe's Motor

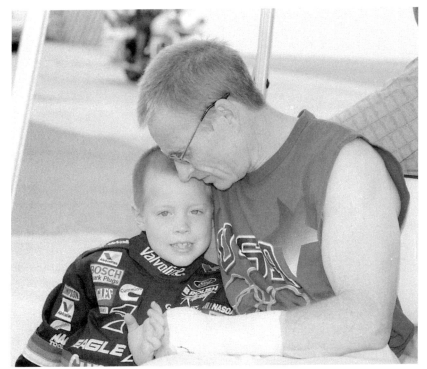

Matt Martin has had the opportunity to learn from the best. **(Photo by Steven Rose/MMP Inc.)**

Speedway. In 1999, he won the Mid-Florida Junior Novice Championships.

In 2002, he set a quarter midget track record at Little New Smyrna, in Florida, and also set a record in his new Bandolero car. In the Summer Shootout Series that year at Lowe's, Matt had one victory, seven top fives and nine top 10s in 10 starts and finished second in points in the Bandolero Bandits series.

He also finished sixth in the nation in Bandoleros.

He has a three-man crew, all from North Florida: Don Pratt, Shane Henry and Glenn Garrison.

Pratt, a few years older than Mark Martin and about 20 years older than Henry and Garrison, once described the surprise of getting his job. "I had to ask him [Mark] to repeat what he'd said [when he called]," Pratt said. "I couldn't believe it.

"Matt's performance is like something you'd read about in a book. You only have to tell him something once. He's a smart kid."

Pratt drives the transporter and helps fabricate parts and maintain the equipment, including the Legends cars.

"He can't race in one until he turns 12," Henry has said, "but he's practiced in one four or five times already. He's already running lap times that are within a couple of tenths of what Mark ran."

Garrison, who went to high school with Henry, also sees something special in Matt: patience. "A lot of kids are a lot rougher out on the race track. Matt will wait until he has a good chance to make a safe pass."

Said friend Wayne Brooks, "The last time I talked to Mark, he said Matt had more talent when he started than he did halfway through his career. So that's really good. Some people have a natural knack for what these old cars need."

The No. 2 Gatorade Bandolero is 47 inches wide, 10 feet, nine inches long and only 34 inches high, but it has a sturdy roll cage, wide tires and a sleek paint job with yellow, orange and green over a black base. The design includes yellow flames, shooting from the front, "just because they're cool," according to Matt.

Matt already is thinking about what he wants to drive next—well, when he's 16. "I want to drive an Eclipse, if they're still in style," he once said. "I want to modify the body, modify the wheels and modify the exhaust so it sings. I want to put a chain around the license plate, and tint the windows dark so you can't see inside it. I want a silver or blue one."

The way his career is headed, he also may want to add a radar detector.

TAYLOR CO., KY.;
MARIETTA, OHIO;
WICHITA, KANSAS;
SELLERSBURG, IND.;
SALT LAKE CITY, UTAH;
AVOCA, IOWA;
PT. PLEASANT, N.J.;
QUEENS, N.Y.

*—A sample of locations on fans' bricks
around the Roush Racing fountain*

Statistics

One time when Mark was just starting out, he, his father, car builder Larry Shaw and friend Banjo Graham were traveling to a race in Anderson, Indiana. "We were working on a race car real late, and we get ready to go and we get in the truck to drive," Shaw said. "We get to somewhere in Illinois, and Mark got back in the back seat, and we took a magic marker and drew Banjo Graham a mustache.

"And we stopped to eat, and we get this waitress to take our order, and the waitress starts laughing. And we go into the bathroom and Banjo looks up in the mirror and sees his face. Mark did some things like that."

But, of course, on the track Mark is serious business. He has won a lot of races through the years, and many consider him to be the best driver who hasn't won a NASCAR Cup championship. These are some of the numbers on the scoreboard.

(Photo by Action Sports Photography Inc.)

Mark Martin Quick Facts

Born: January 9, 1959

Where: Batesville, Arkansas

Spouse: Arlene; they were married in October of 1984.

Children: Amy, Rachel, Heather, Stacy and Matthew.

Residence: Daytona Beach, Florida

(Photo by Action Sports Photography Inc.)

Track Facts
(Prior to 2004 Season)

Victories: 33 (fourth among active drivers)

Top five finishes: More than 200

Top 10 finishes: More than 300

Consecutive starts: More than 500 NASCAR NEXTEL Cup races, dating to February 18, 1988

Finish in 2003: 17th

Mark, prior to an IROC event. (Photo by Action Sports Photography Inc.)

Mark's Car

Wheelbase: 110"
Treadwidth: 60" (center to center)
Height: 51"
Overall Length: 16'5"
Weight: (without driver) 3400 lbs. minimum
Weight Distribution: 1800 lbs. (left); 1600 lbs. (right) (minimums)

SPONSORSHIP
Primary: Pfizer

EQUIPMENT
Engine: 358 cubic-inch Ford V-8
Carburetor: Holley
Ignition: MSD
Ignition wires: MSD
Spark plugs: BOSCH
Transmission: Roush Racing
Battery: Reactor Cell
Camshaft: Competition Cams
Pistons: Wiseco/Roush Racing
Valves: Xceldyne
Connecting Rods: Carrillo

Crankshaft: Moldex/Bryant
Engine Bearings: Michigan Clevite
Shifter Linkage: Hurst
Headers: Roush Racing/Reinhart
Clutch: Quartermaster
Gasoline: Sunoco
Oil System: Roush Racing
Engine Oil: Pennzoil
Oil Filters: Wix
Fuel Cell: ATL (22 gallons)
Axles: Speedway Engineering
Wheels: AERO (10" width, 15" diameter)
Tires: Goodyear Eagle Racing Tires
Brakes: Brembo
Shock Absorbers: Penske
Hose Ends & Fittings: Aeroquip
Rear Suspension: 9" Ford Rear End Housing
Bellhousing: Ford
Belts: Goodyear
Gauges: Autometer

SAFETY

Helmet: Arai
Safety Belts: Simpson
Fire Extinguisher: Fire Bottle Safety System
Window Net: Simpson

Mark's Crew

Drew Blickensderfer: Rear Tire Changer
Scott Bowen: Front Tire Carrier
Eddie Clowers: Pit Support
Jim Davis: Mechanic/Tire Specialist
Jonathan Decosta: Second Gas/Pit Support
Danny Eklund: Mechanic/Catch Can
John Goodman: Sign/Pit Support
Gene Hopkins Jr.: Mechanic/Pit Support
Rick Machcinski: Engine Tuner/Gasman
Mark Martin: Driver
Harry McMullen: General Manager
Dale Merwin: Pit Support
Bob Osborne: Chief Engineer
Ed Pardue: Shock Specialist/Spotter
Will Smith: Rear Suspension/Rear Tire Carrier
Bart Starr: Truck Driver/Tire Catcher
Adam Taylor: Fuel Runner
Pat Tryson: Crew Chief
Chris Webb: Mechanic & Wiring/Jackman
Kevin Woods: Account Manager
Todd Zeigler: Car Chief/Front Tire Changer

Quick Career Rewind

1977: American Speed Association (ASA) Rookie of the Year.

1978, 1979, 1980, 1986: Won the ASA championship each year.

1981: Running as driver/owner, Mark competed in five NASCAR Winston Cup races and ended the season 42nd in points.

1982: Competed a full season as a driver/owner and was runner-up to Geoffrey Bodine for Rookie of the Year. He had eight top 10s running without a sponsor.

1983: Ran one race with his own team, then auctioned off everything in his shop.

1984-1986: Returned to ASA.

1987: Ran the NASCAR Busch Series.

1988: Joined Jack Roush and Roush Racing in a move that would fast-forward his career; he was 15th in points, had 10 top 10s and three top fives, with a second place at Bristol and a pole at Dover.

1989: Mark got his first career victory at Rockingham.

1990, 1994, 1998, 2002: Finished second in NASCAR Cup points.

2001: Won two poles and finished 12th in points; at the end of the season, the team welcomed a new crew chief, Ben Leslie.

2002: Mark was second in championship points, 38 behind Tony Stewart; he also won the May race at Lowe's Motor Speedway near Charlotte to break a 73-race winless streak. He had 22 top 10 finishes, to tie for the lead in that category with rookie Ryan Newman.

2003: Finished 17th overall in NASCAR points with winnings over $4 million. Pat Tryson became Mark's crew chief during the last two races of 2003.

(Photo by Action Sports Photography Inc.)

The Next Generation

Matt Martin

What he does: Races a No. 66 Gatorade Ford F-150.

Birthdate: December 17, 1991

When his career began: Racing quarter midgets at age seven in 1999.

Favorite sponsor: Gatorade

Favorite flavor of it: Kiwi

Favorite school subject: Math

If he wasn't a race driver he'd: Play football

On beating his dad in a Legends car: "He didn't know how to go fast. He's a pretty good driver at NASCAR. I couldn't beat him at NASCAR, but he couldn't beat me in smaller cars. He's pretty good, but I'm good, too."

The future: Matt, at age 11, signed a sponsorship deal with the Ford Motor Company, the youngest driver the company sponsors.

(Photo by Action Sports Photography Inc.)

Celebrate the Heroes of Auto Racing
in These Other Releases from Sports Publishing!